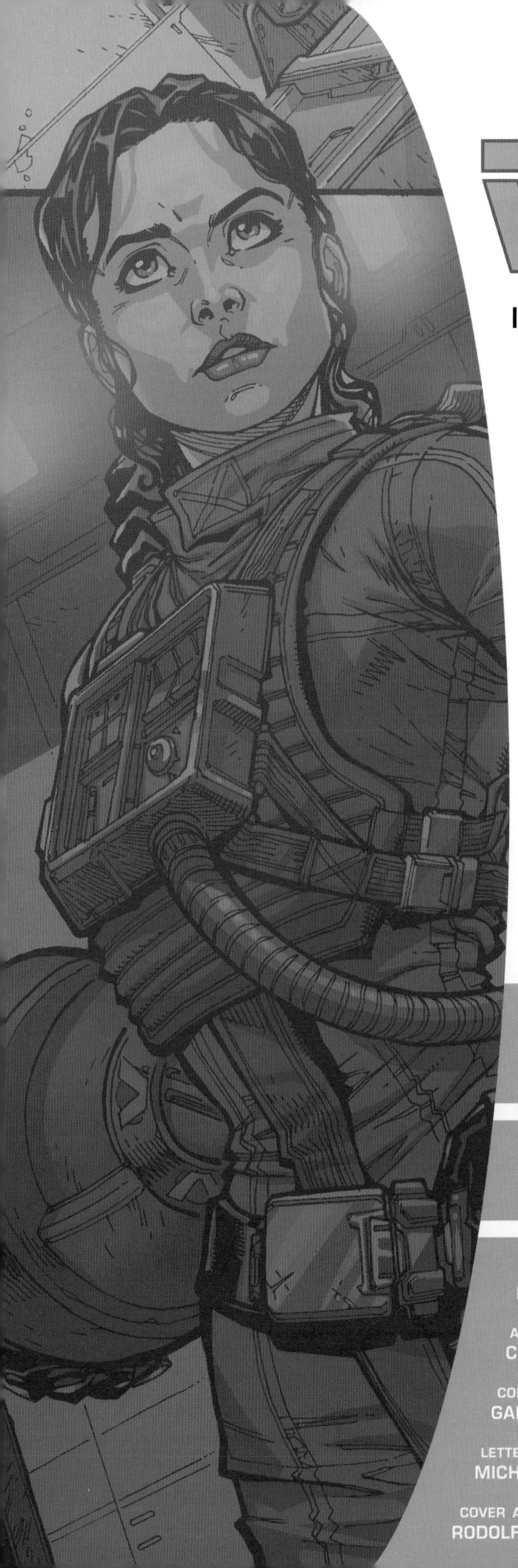

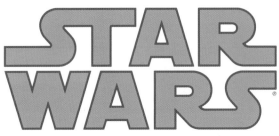

STAR WARS®

IN THE SHADOW OF YAVIN
VOLUME FIVE

After their resupply mission for the Rebel Alliance is exposed to the Empire, Han Solo and Chewbacca seek refuge in the Coruscant underworld, where they are being hunted by Boba Fett. Meanwhile, at the construction site of the second Death Star, Darth Vader, having fallen from the Emperor's favor, finds an unexpected ally in the Force . . .

Luke Skywalker, who has been grounded for breaking mission protocol, receives a warning from the ghost of Ben Kenobi—which prompts him to further disobey orders . . .

And Princess Leia and her elite X-wing squadron are cornered by Colonel Bircher's Star Destroyers and his TIE Interceptor group—forcing Leia and her pilots to make a stand . . . possibly their last.

THE REBELLION
FROM THE BATTLE OF YAVIN
TO FIVE YEARS AFTER

The events in this story take place shortly after the events in *Star Wars:* Episode IV—*A New Hope.*

SCRIPT
BRIAN WOOD

ART
CARLOS D'ANDA

COLORS
GABE ELTAEB

LETTERING
MICHAEL HEISLER

COVER ART
RODOLFO MIGLIARI

DARK HORSE COMICS

WWW.ABDOPUBLISHING.COM

Reinforced library bound edition published in 2015 by Spotlight, a division of ABDO
PO Box 398166, Minneapolis, Minnesota 55439. Spotlight produces high-quality
reinforced library bound editions for schools and libraries. Published by agreement
with Dark Horse Comics, Inc., and Lucasfilm Ltd.

Printed in the United States of America, North Mankato, Minnesota.
052014
072014

THIS BOOK CONTAINS
RECYCLED MATERIALS

LIBRARY OF CONGRESS CATALOGING-IN-PUBLICATION DATA

Wood, Brian, 1972-
   Star Wars : in the shadow of Yavin / writer: Brian Wood ; artist: Carlos D'Anda. --
Reinforced library bound edition.
      pages cm.
   "Dark Horse."
   "LucasFilm."
   ISBN 978-1-61479-286-4 (vol. 1) -- ISBN 978-1-61479-287-1 (vol. 2) -- ISBN 978-1-
61479-288-8 (vol. 3) -- ISBN 978-1-61479-289-5 (vol. 4) -- ISBN 978-1-61479-290-1
(vol. 5) -- ISBN 978-1-61479-291-8 (vol. 6)
1. Graphic novels. I. D'Anda, Carlos, illustrator. II. Dark Horse Comics. III. Lucasfilm,
Ltd. IV. Title. V. Title: In the shadow of Yavin.
   PZ7.7.W65St 2015
   741.5'973--dc23

                              2014005383

Spotlight

A Division of ABDO
www.abdopublishing.com

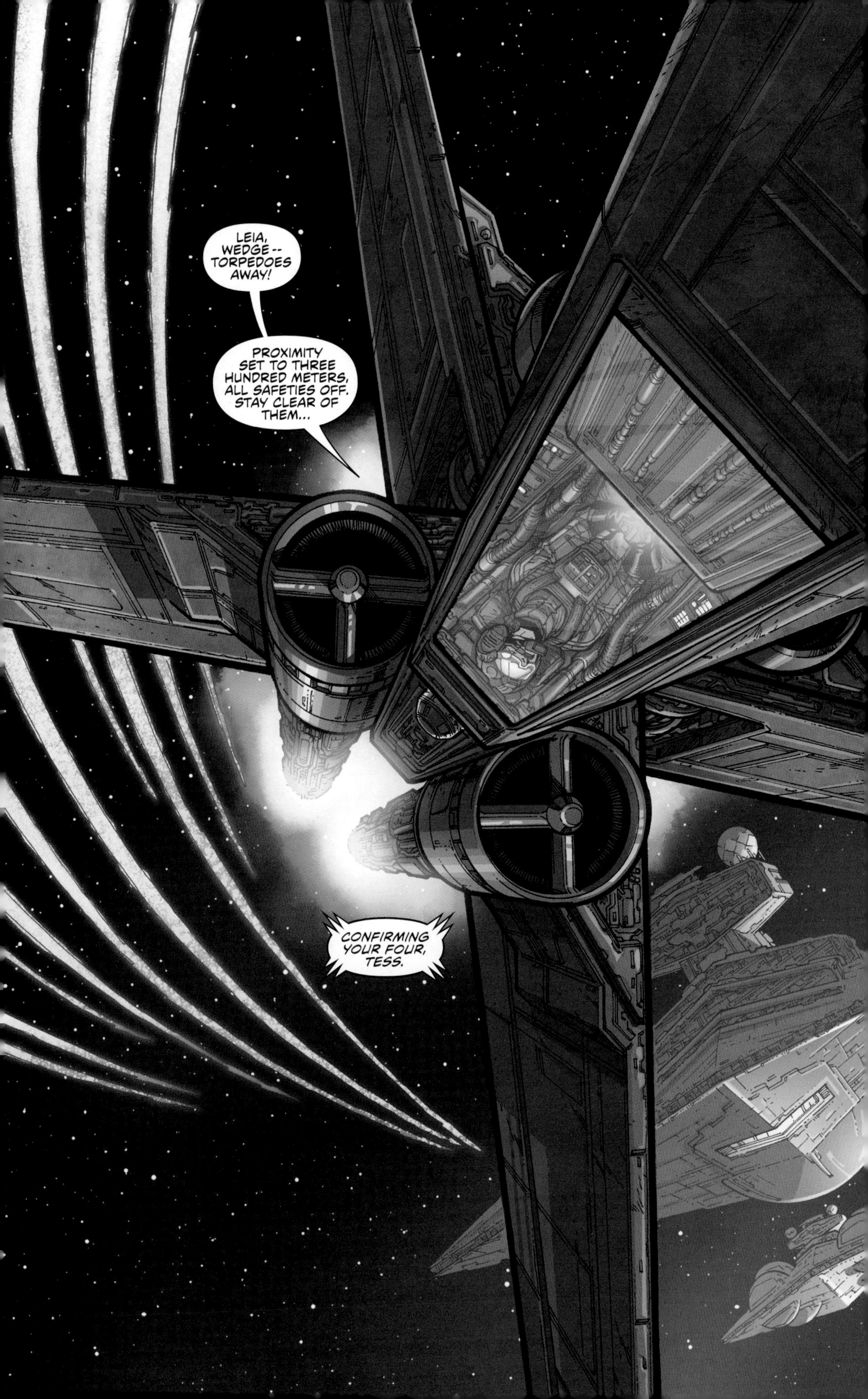
LEIA, WEDGE-- TORPEDOES AWAY!
PROXIMITY SET TO THREE HUNDRED METERS, ALL SAFETIES OFF. STAY CLEAR OF THEM...
CONFIRMING YOUR FOUR, TESS.

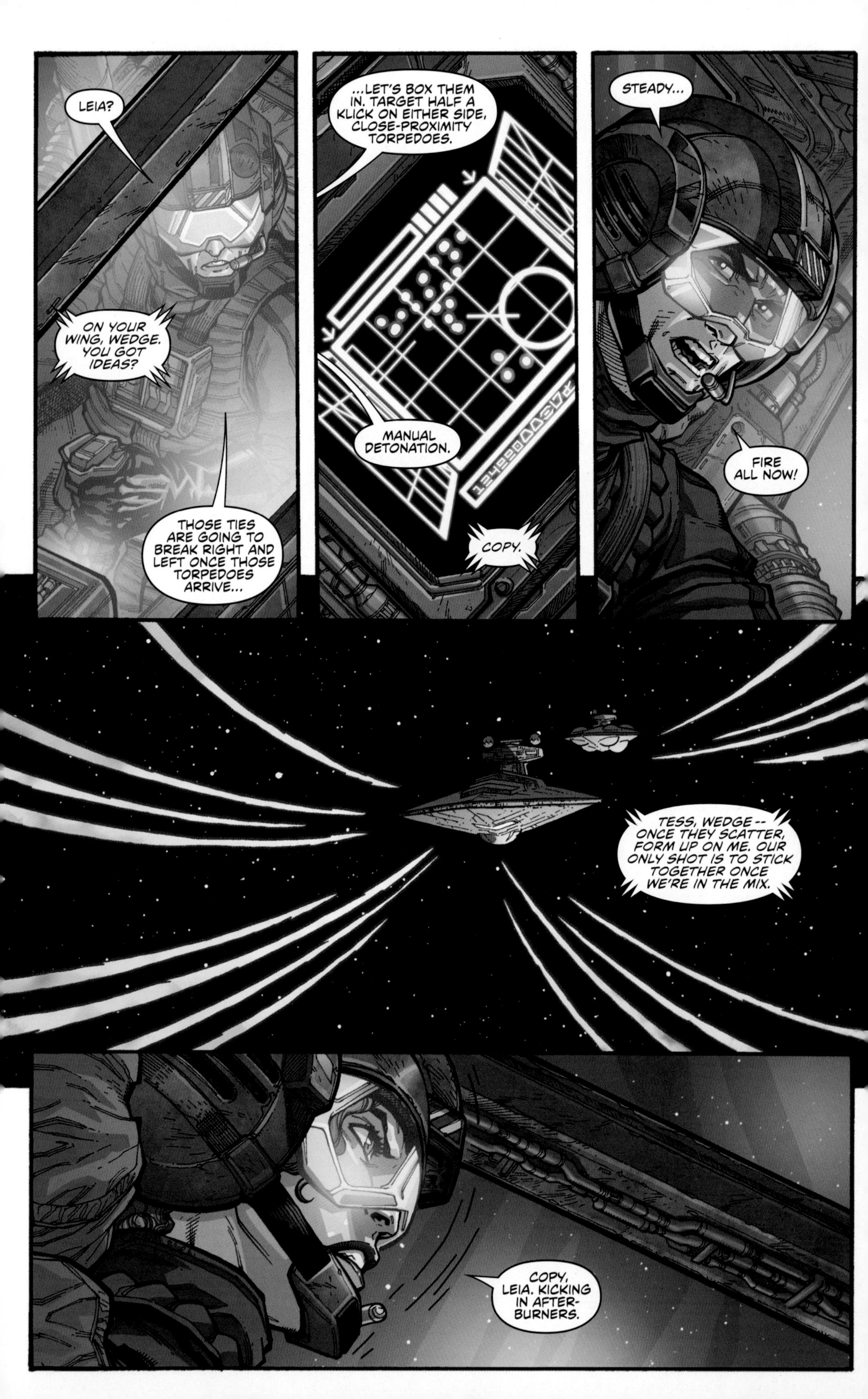
LEIA?
ON YOUR WING, WEDGE. YOU GOT IDEAS?
THOSE TIES ARE GOING TO BREAK RIGHT AND LEFT ONCE THOSE TORPEDOES ARRIVE...
...LET'S BOX THEM IN. TARGET HALF A KLICK ON EITHER SIDE, CLOSE-PROXIMITY TORPEDOES.
MANUAL DETONATION.
COPY.
STEADY...
FIRE ALL NOW!
TESS, WEDGE -- ONCE THEY SCATTER, FORM UP ON ME. OUR ONLY SHOT IS TO STICK TOGETHER ONCE WE'RE IN THE MIX.
COPY, LEIA. KICKING IN AFTER-BURNERS.

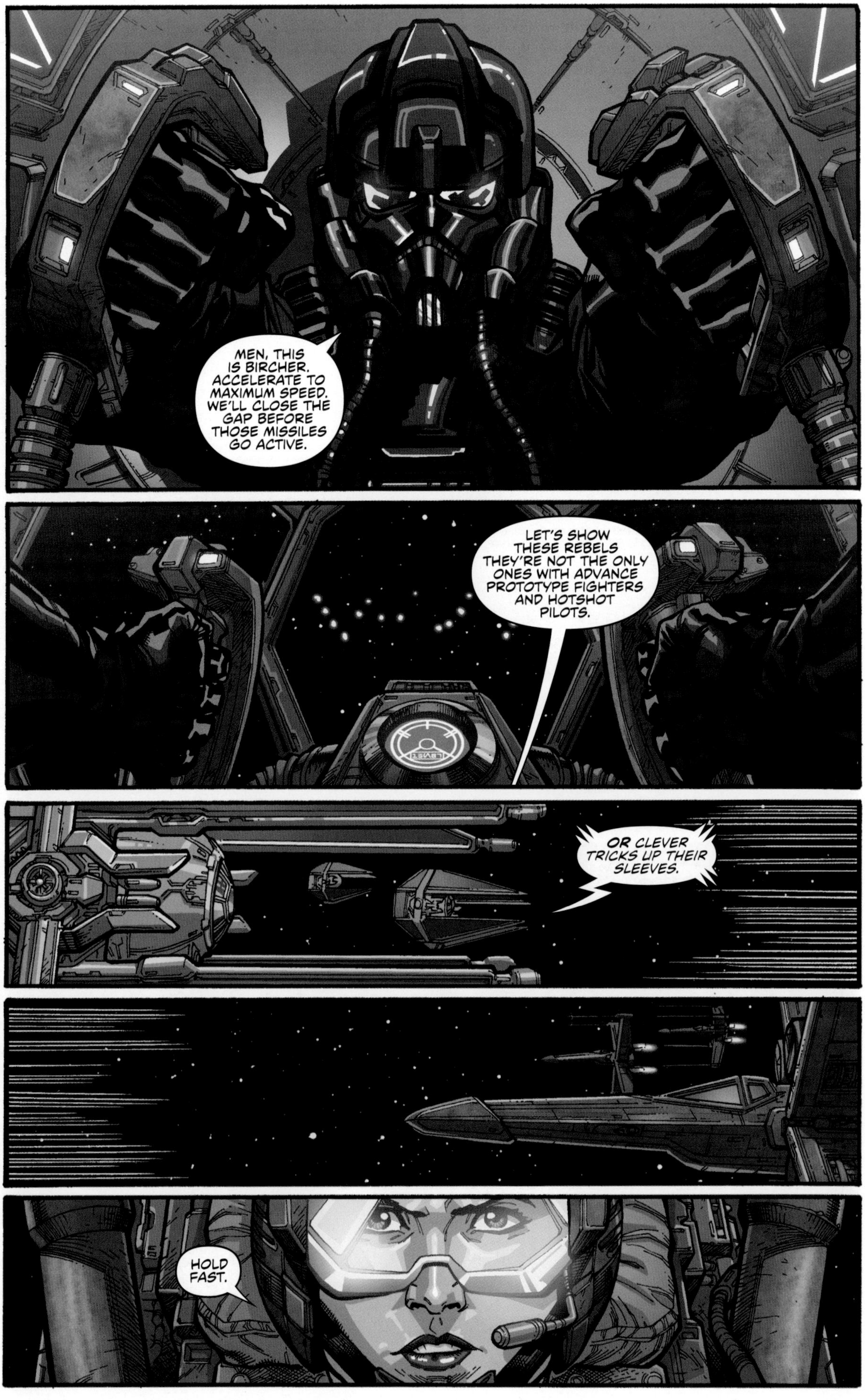
MEN, THIS IS BIRCHER. ACCELERATE TO MAXIMUM SPEED. WE'LL CLOSE THE GAP BEFORE THOSE MISSILES GO ACTIVE.
LET'S SHOW THESE REBELS THEY'RE NOT THE ONLY ONES WITH ADVANCE PROTOTYPE FIGHTERS AND HOTSHOT PILOTS.
OR CLEVER TRICKS UP THEIR SLEEVES.
HOLD FAST.

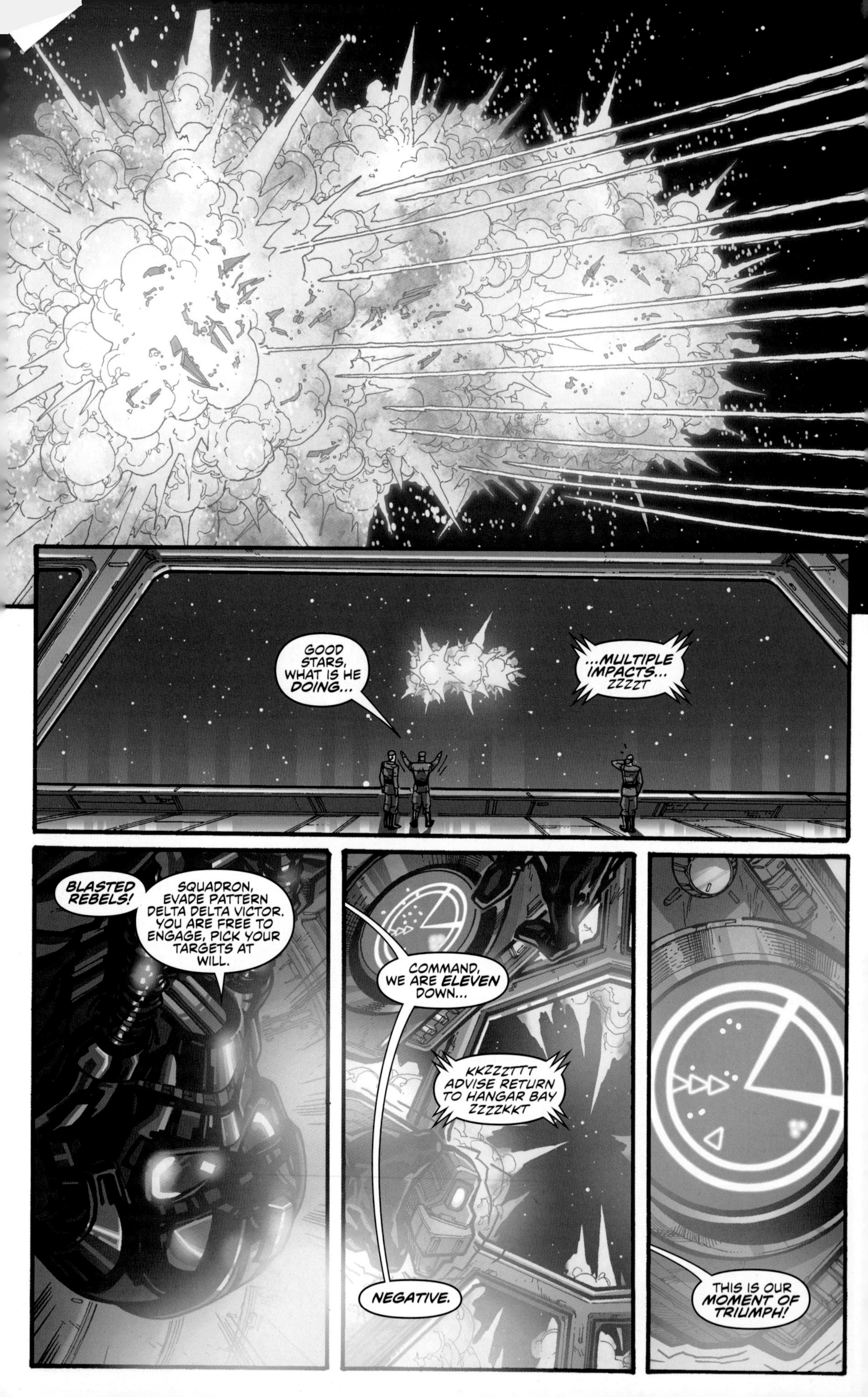
GOOD STARS, WHAT IS HE DOING...
...MULTIPLE IMPACTS... ZZZZT
BLASTED REBELS!
SQUADRON, EVADE PATTERN DELTA DELTA VICTOR. YOU ARE FREE TO ENGAGE, PICK YOUR TARGETS AT WILL.
COMMAND, WE ARE ELEVEN DOWN...
KKZZZTTT ADVISE RETURN TO HANGAR BAY ZZZZKKT
NEGATIVE.
THIS IS OUR MOMENT OF TRIUMPH!

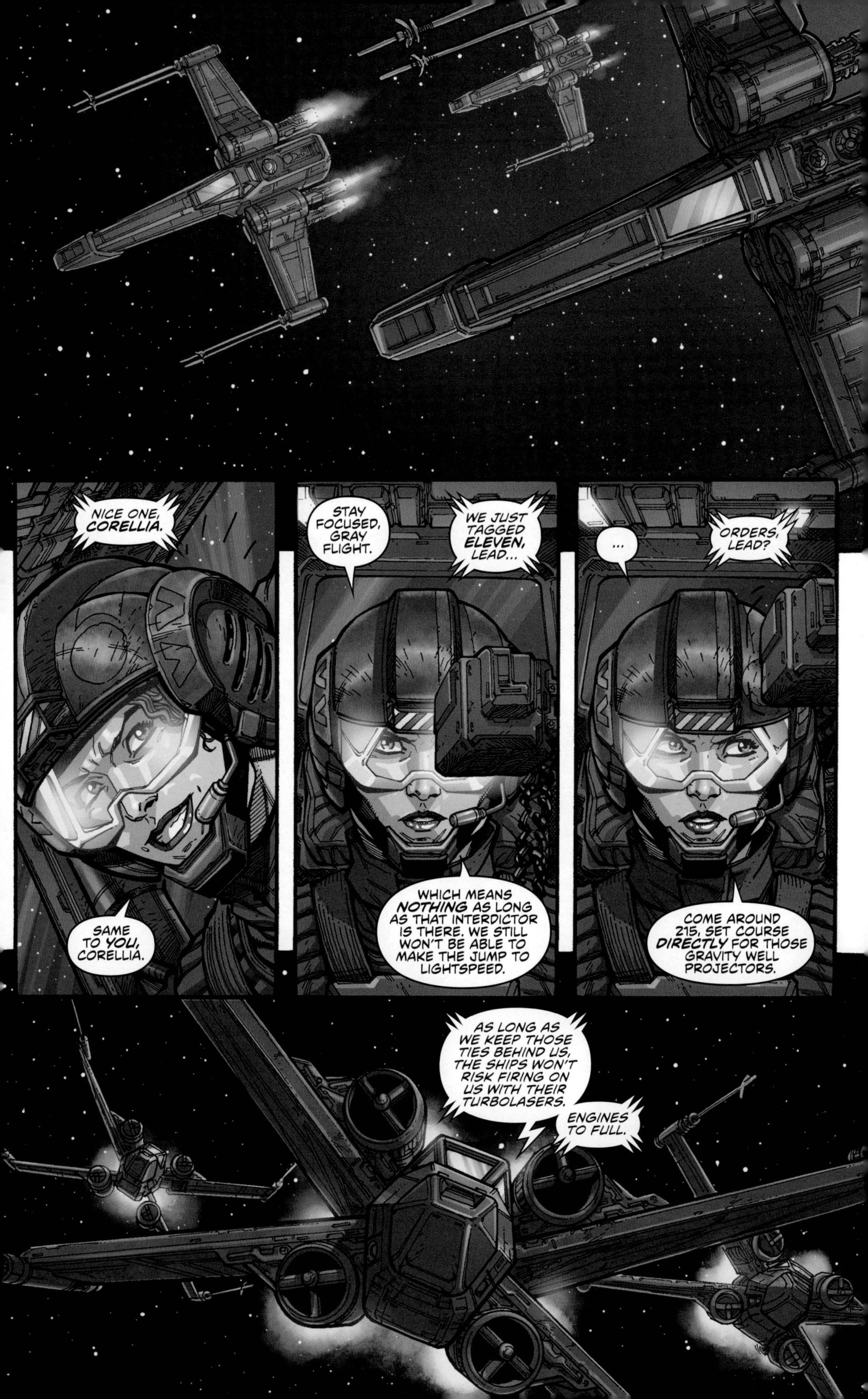
NICE ONE, CORELLIA.
SAME TO YOU, CORELLIA.
STAY FOCUSED, GRAY FLIGHT.
WE JUST TAGGED ELEVEN, LEAD...
WHICH MEANS NOTHING AS LONG AS THAT INTERDICTOR IS THERE. WE STILL WON'T BE ABLE TO MAKE THE JUMP TO LIGHTSPEED.
...
ORDERS, LEAD?
COME AROUND 215, SET COURSE DIRECTLY FOR THOSE GRAVITY WELL PROJECTORS.
AS LONG AS WE KEEP THOSE TIES BEHIND US, THE SHIPS WON'T RISK FIRING ON US WITH THEIR TURBOLASERS.
ENGINES TO FULL.

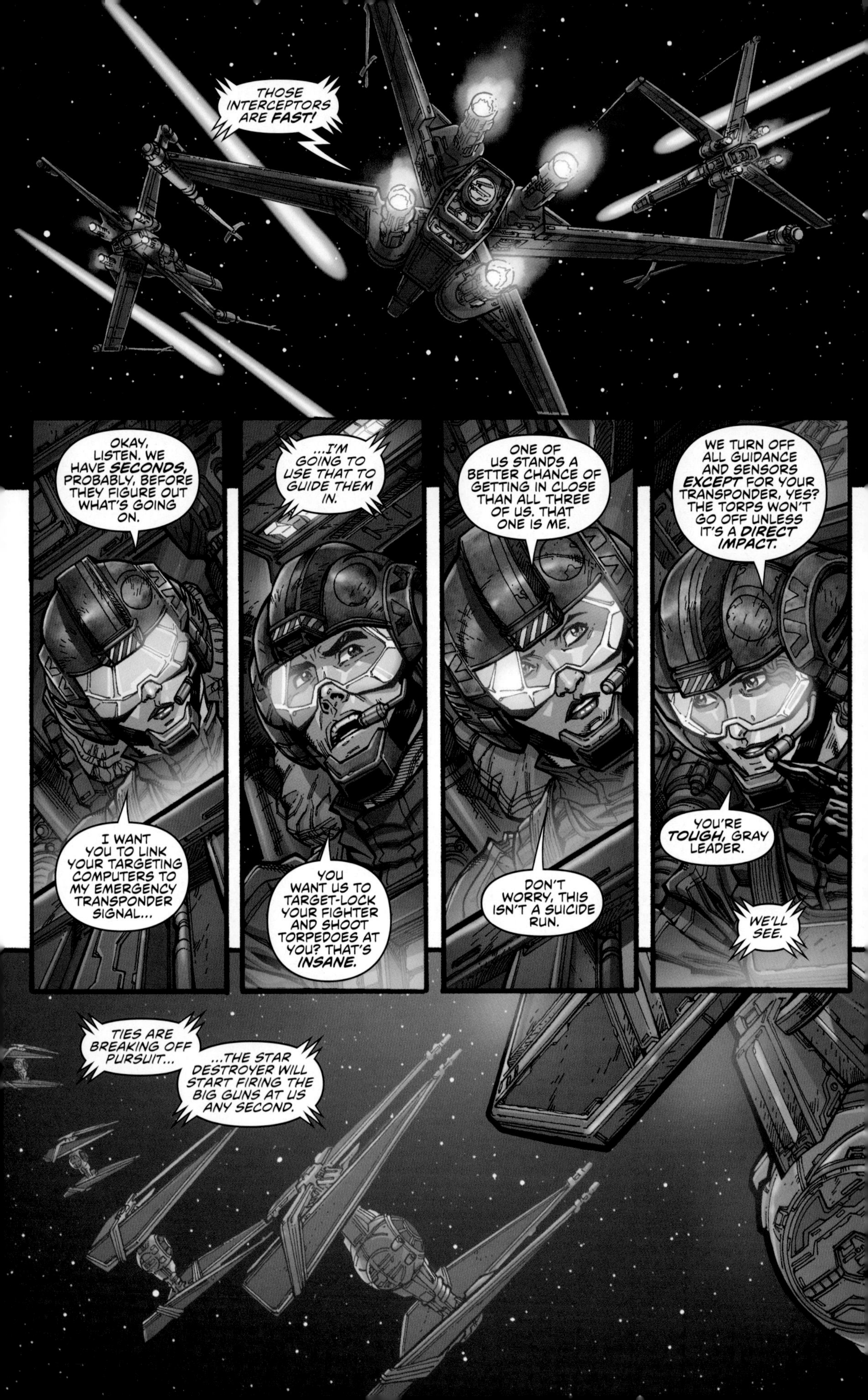
THOSE INTERCEPTORS ARE FAST!
OKAY, LISTEN. WE HAVE SECONDS, PROBABLY, BEFORE THEY FIGURE OUT WHAT'S GOING ON.
I WANT YOU TO LINK YOUR TARGETING COMPUTERS TO MY EMERGENCY TRANSPONDER SIGNAL...
...I'M GOING TO USE THAT TO GUIDE THEM IN.
YOU WANT US TO TARGET-LOCK YOUR FIGHTER AND SHOOT TORPEDOES AT YOU? THAT'S INSANE.
ONE OF US STANDS A BETTER CHANCE OF GETTING IN CLOSE THAN ALL THREE OF US. THAT ONE IS ME.
DON'T WORRY, THIS ISN'T A SUICIDE RUN.
WE TURN OFF ALL GUIDANCE AND SENSORS EXCEPT FOR YOUR TRANSPONDER, YES? THE TORPS WON'T GO OFF UNLESS IT'S A DIRECT IMPACT.
YOU'RE TOUGH, GRAY LEADER.
WE'LL SEE.
TIES ARE BREAKING OFF PURSUIT...
...THE STAR DESTROYER WILL START FIRING THE BIG GUNS AT US ANY SECOND.

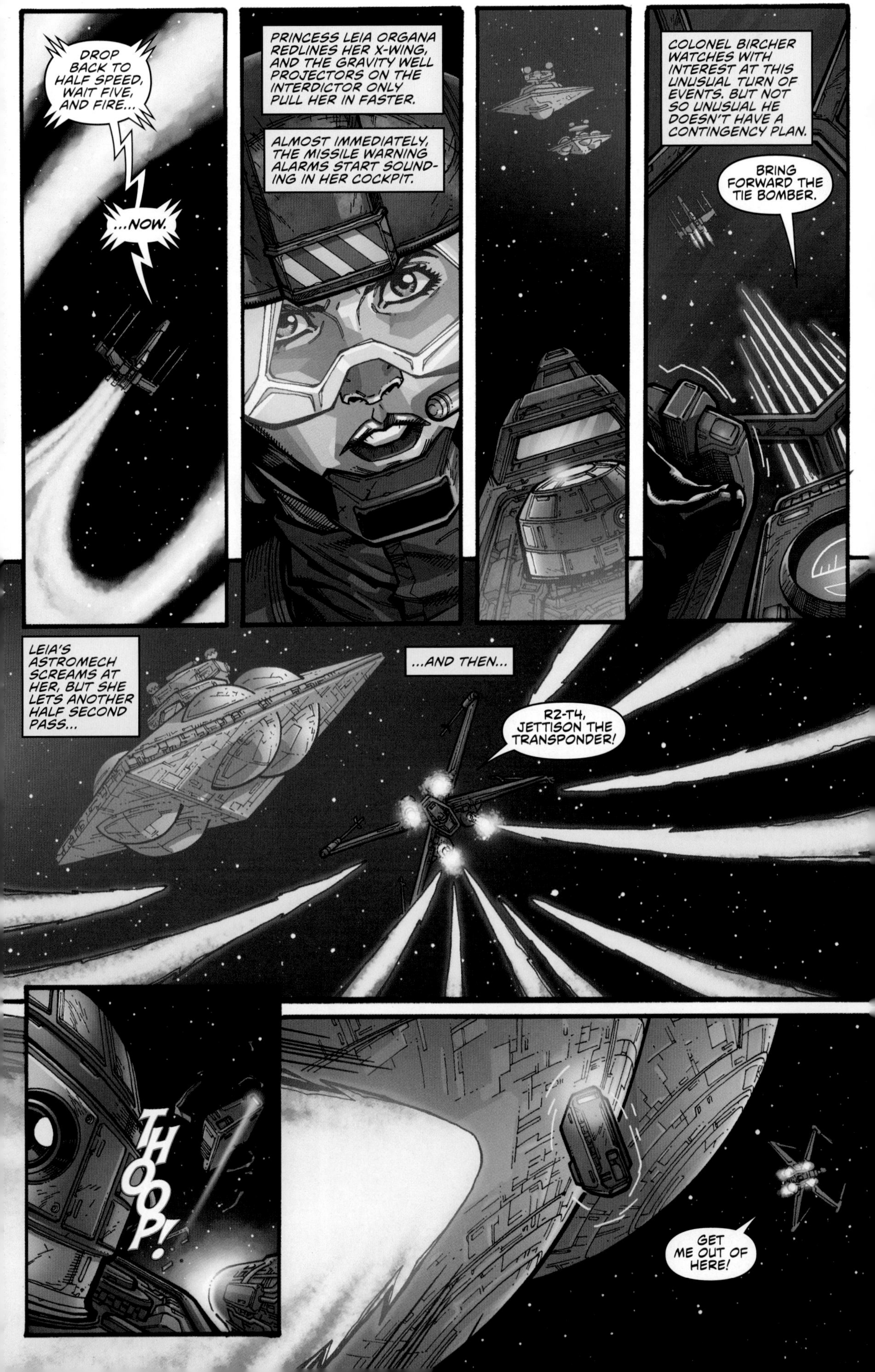
DROP BACK TO HALF SPEED, WAIT FIVE, AND FIRE...
...NOW.
PRINCESS LEIA ORGANA REDLINES HER X-WING, AND THE GRAVITY WELL PROJECTORS ON THE INTERDICTOR ONLY PULL HER IN FASTER.
ALMOST IMMEDIATELY, THE MISSILE WARNING ALARMS START SOUNDING IN HER COCKPIT.
COLONEL BIRCHER WATCHES WITH INTEREST AT THIS UNUSUAL TURN OF EVENTS. BUT NOT SO UNUSUAL HE DOESN'T HAVE A CONTINGENCY PLAN.
BRING FORWARD THE TIE BOMBER.
LEIA'S ASTROMECH SCREAMS AT HER, BUT SHE LETS ANOTHER HALF SECOND PASS...
...AND THEN...
R2-T4, JETTISON THE TRANSPONDER!
THOOP!
GET ME OUT OF HERE!

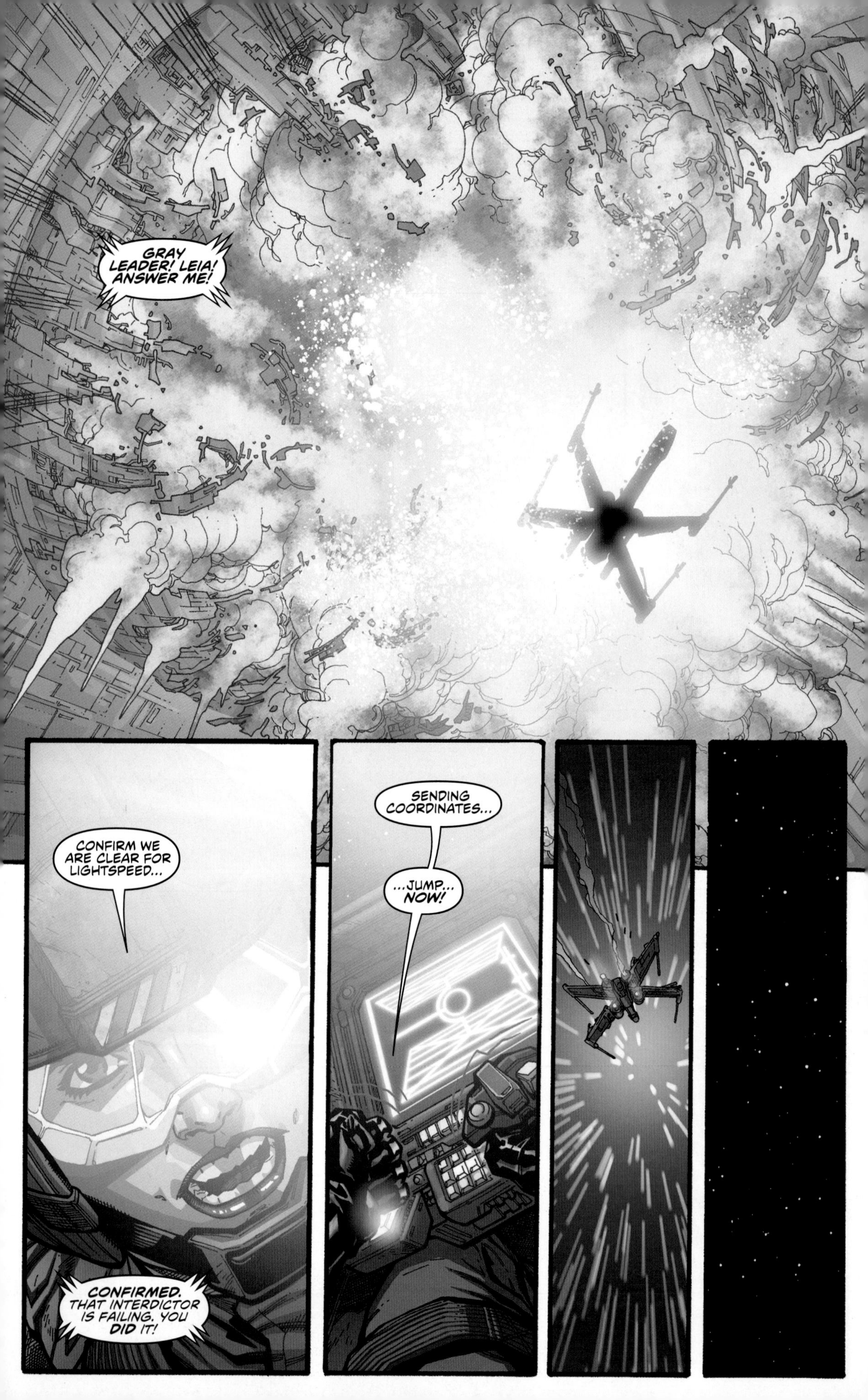
GRAY LEADER! LEIA! ANSWER ME!
CONFIRM WE ARE CLEAR FOR LIGHTSPEED...
CONFIRMED. THAT INTERDICTOR IS FAILING. YOU DID IT!
SENDING COORDINATES...
...JUMP... NOW!

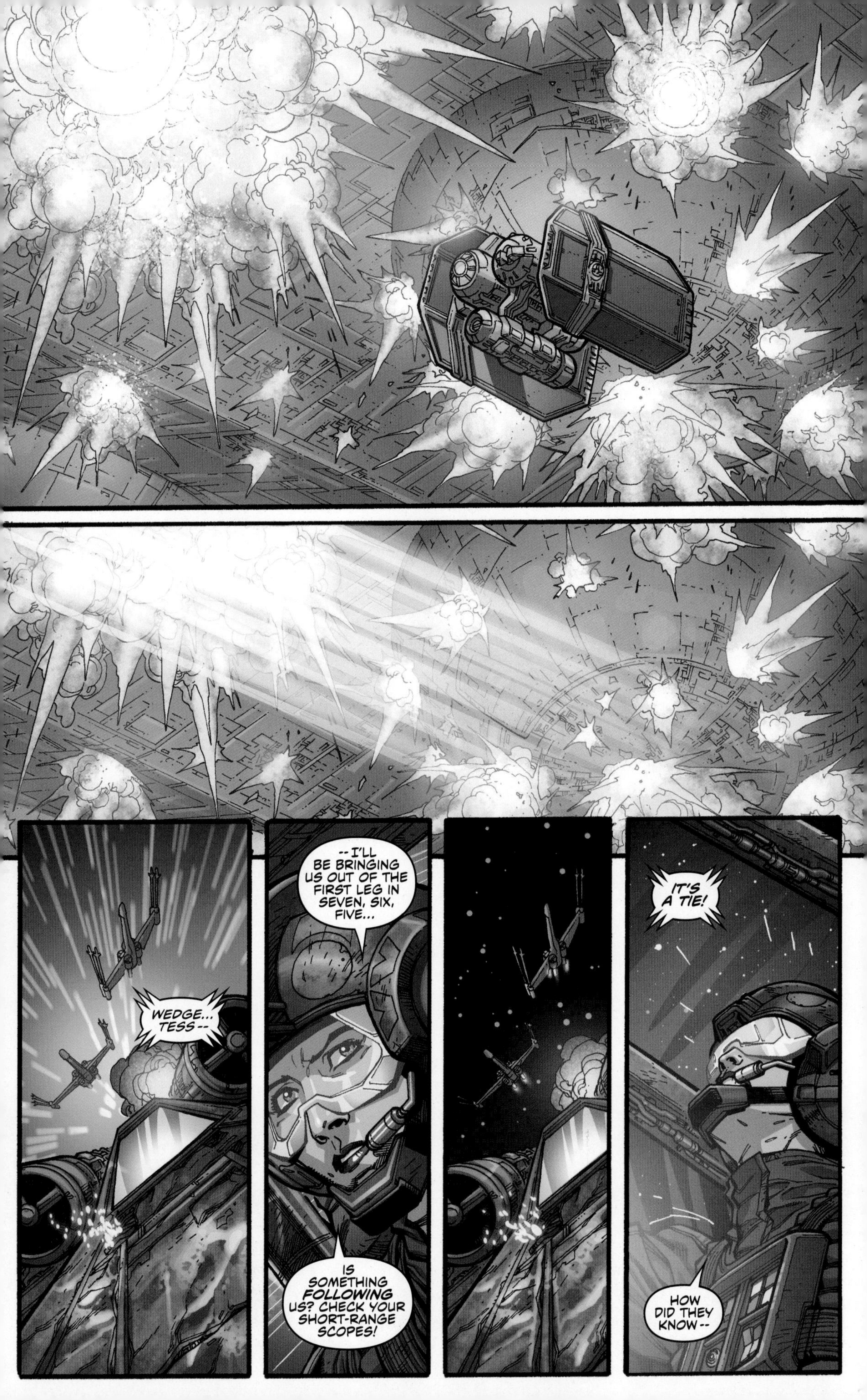
WEDGE... TESS --
-- I'LL BE BRINGING US OUT OF THE FIRST LEG IN SEVEN, SIX, FIVE...
IS SOMETHING FOLLOWING US? CHECK YOUR SHORT-RANGE SCOPES!
IT'S A TIE!
HOW DID THEY KNOW --

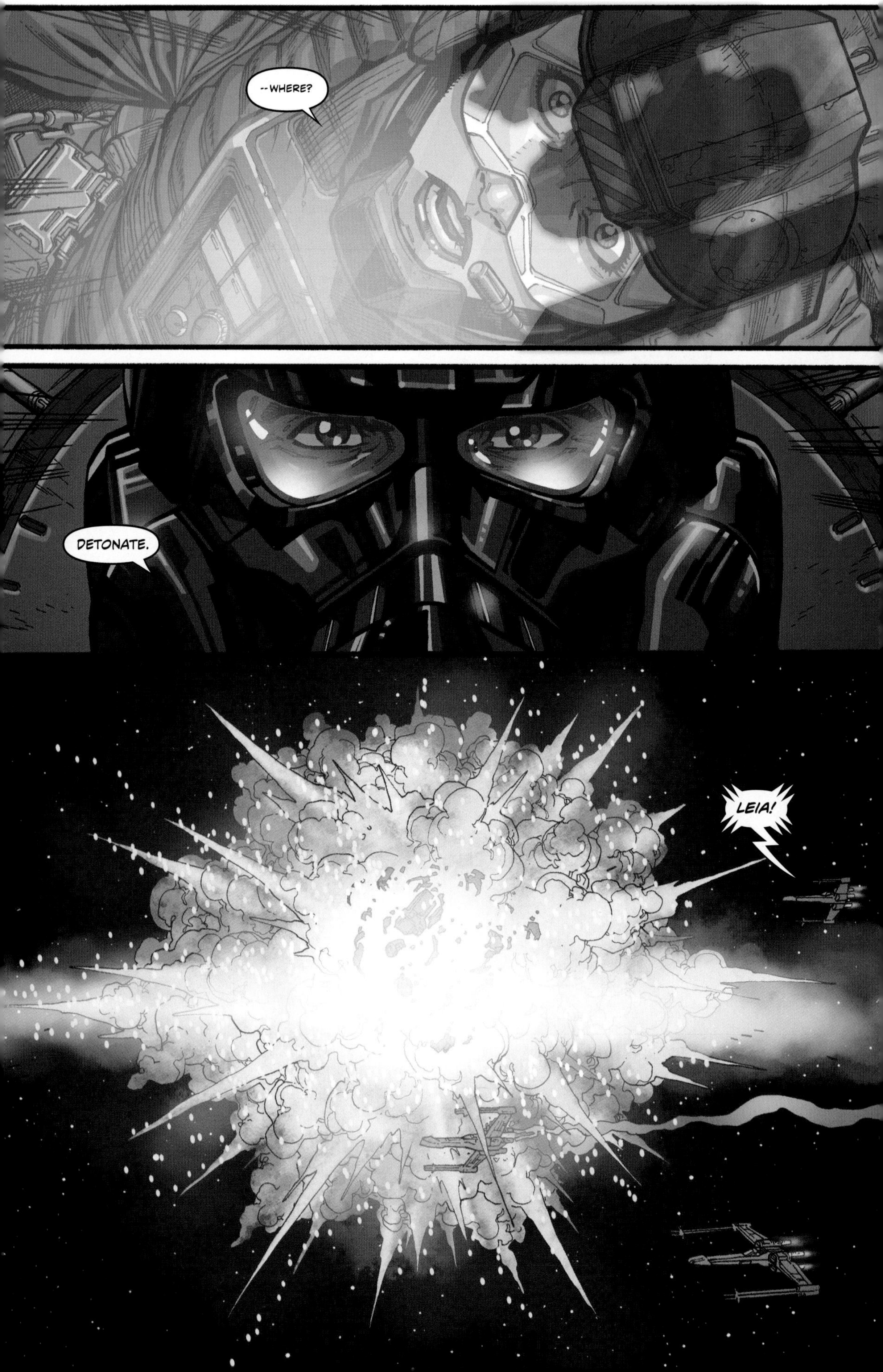
--WHERE?
DETONATE.
LEIA!

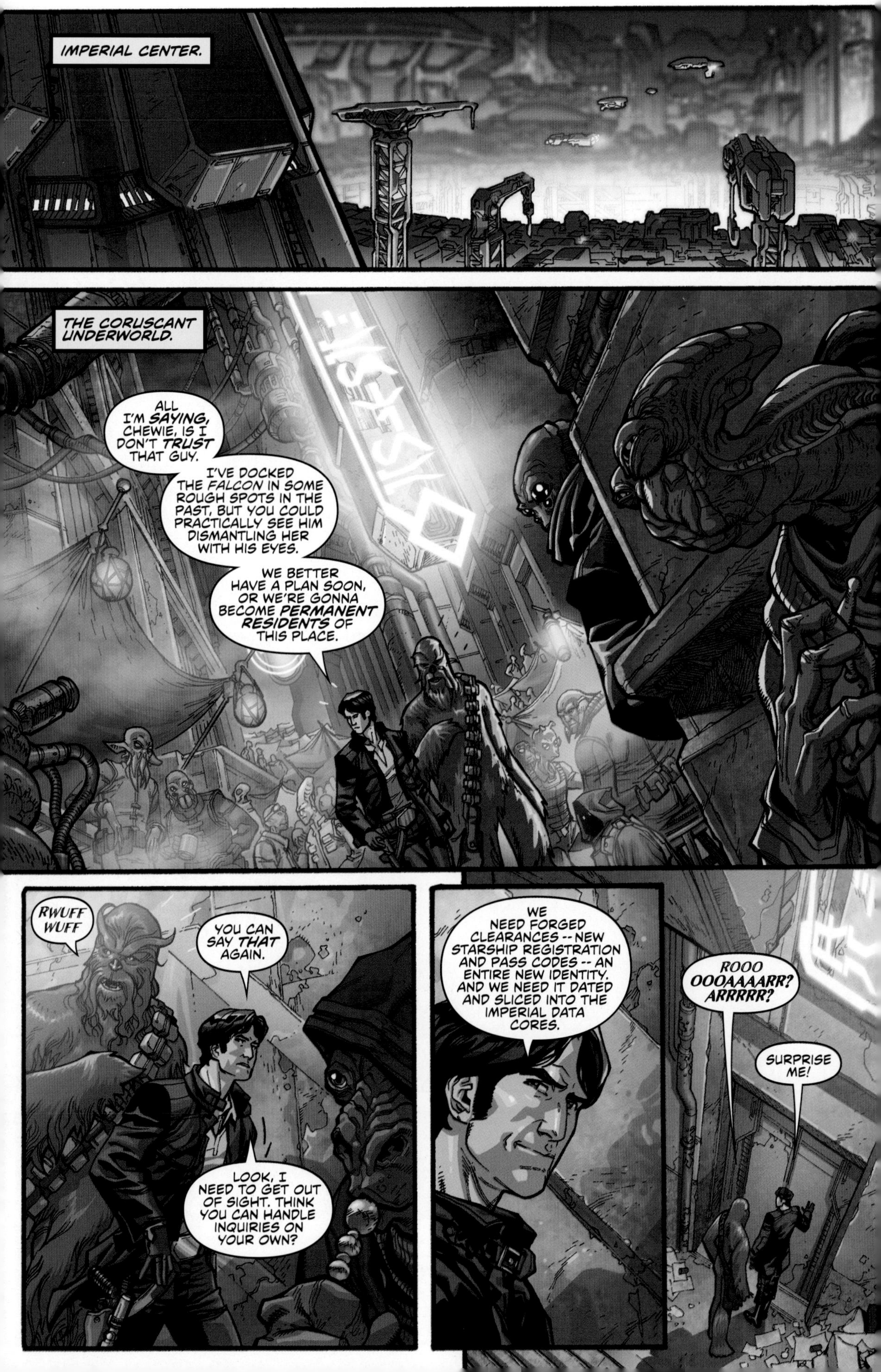
IMPERIAL CENTER.
THE CORUSCANT UNDERWORLD.
ALL I'M SAYING, CHEWIE, IS I DON'T TRUST THAT GUY.
I'VE DOCKED THE FALCON IN SOME ROUGH SPOTS IN THE PAST, BUT YOU COULD PRACTICALLY SEE HIM DISMANTLING HER WITH HIS EYES.
WE BETTER HAVE A PLAN SOON, OR WE'RE GONNA BECOME PERMANENT RESIDENTS OF THIS PLACE.
RWUFF WUFF
YOU CAN SAY THAT AGAIN.
LOOK, I NEED TO GET OUT OF SIGHT. THINK YOU CAN HANDLE INQUIRIES ON YOUR OWN?
WE NEED FORGED CLEARANCES -- NEW STARSHIP REGISTRATION AND PASS CODES -- AN ENTIRE NEW IDENTITY. AND WE NEED IT DATED AND SLICED INTO THE IMPERIAL DATA CORES.
ROOO OOOAAAARR? ARRRRR?
SURPRISE ME!

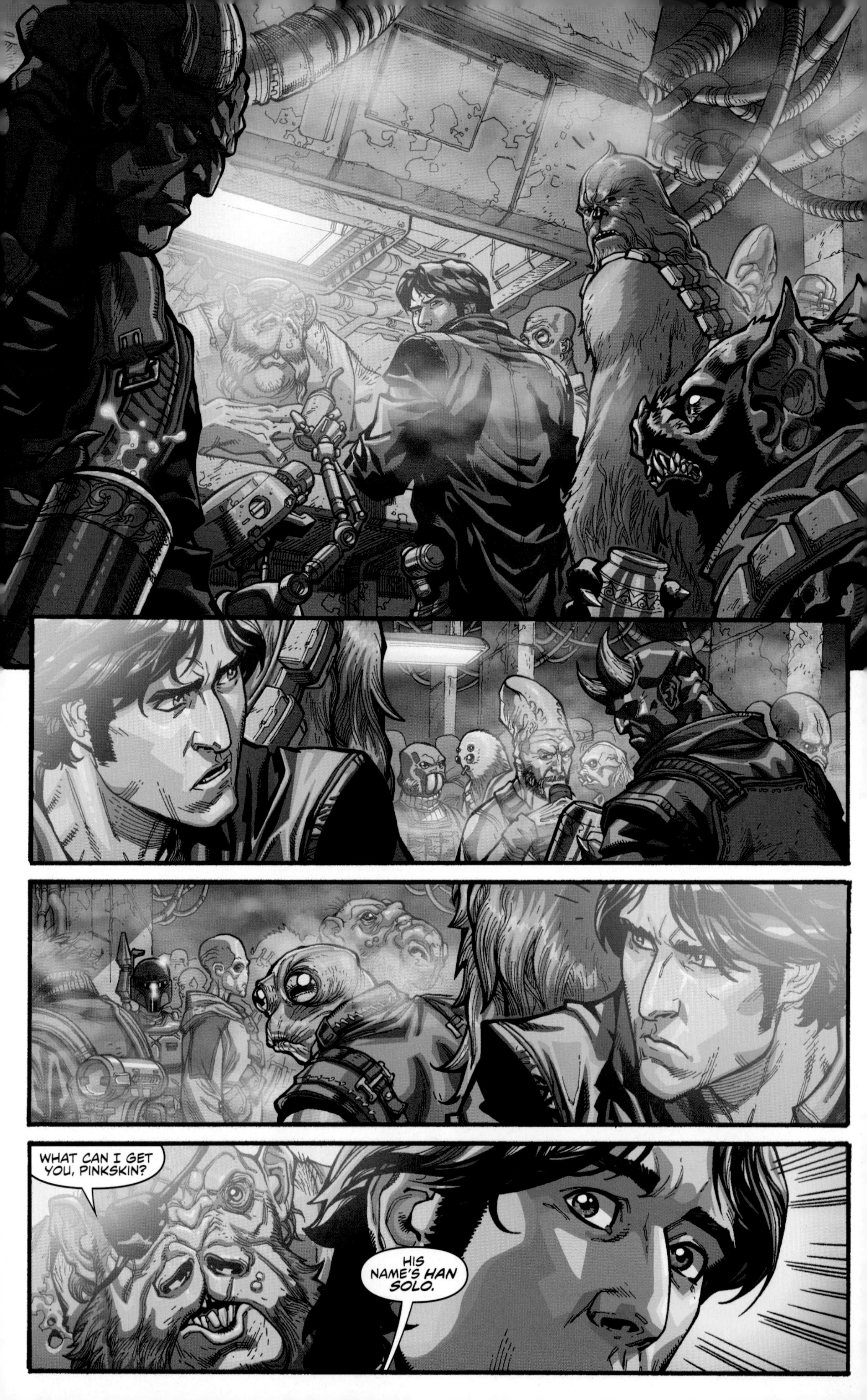
WHAT CAN I GET YOU, PINKSKIN?
HIS NAME'S HAN SOLO.

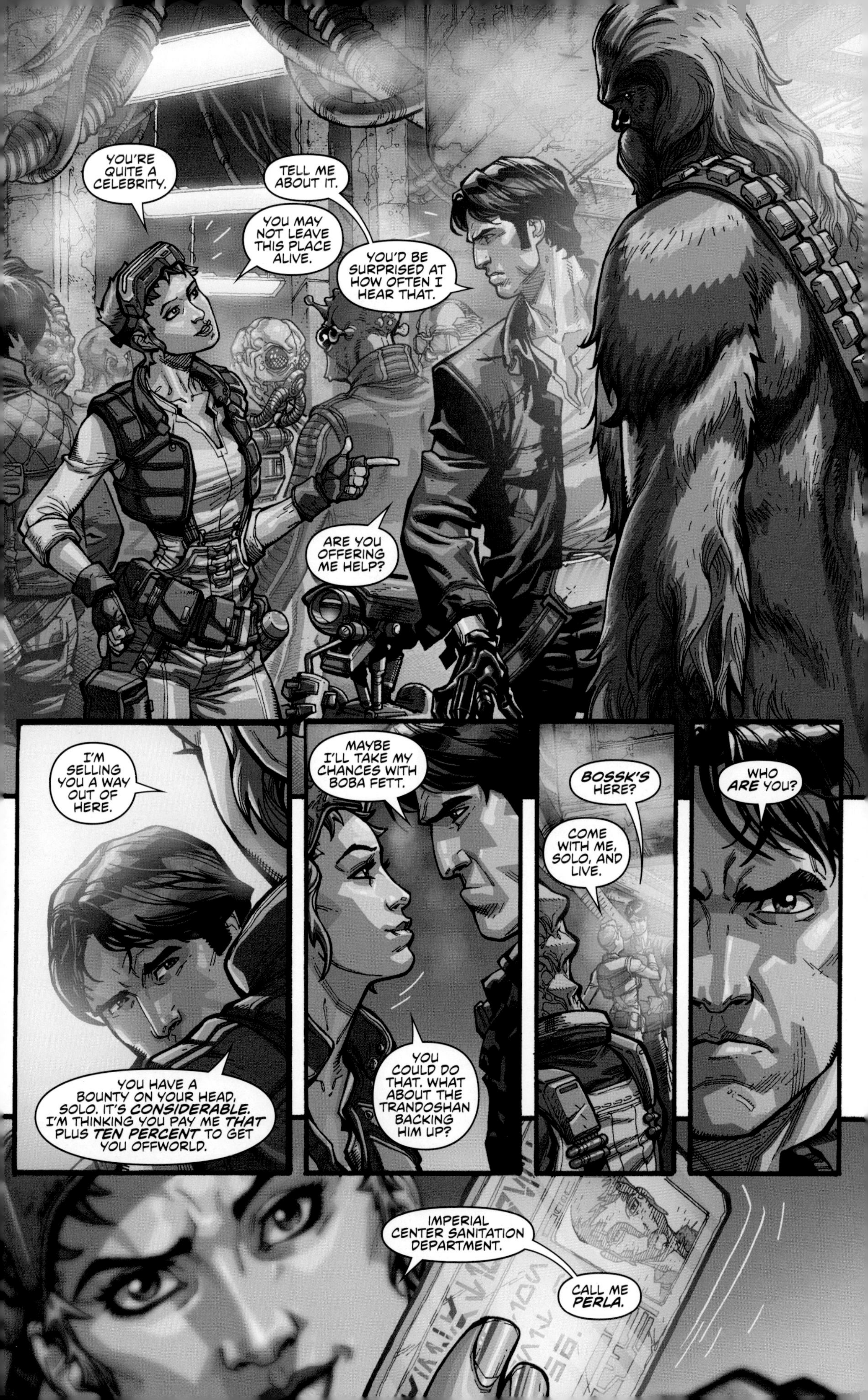
YOU'RE QUITE A CELEBRITY.
TELL ME ABOUT IT.
YOU MAY NOT LEAVE THIS PLACE ALIVE.
YOU'D BE SURPRISED AT HOW OFTEN I HEAR THAT.
ARE YOU OFFERING ME HELP?
I'M SELLING YOU A WAY OUT OF HERE.
YOU HAVE A BOUNTY ON YOUR HEAD, SOLO. IT'S *CONSIDERABLE*. I'M THINKING YOU PAY ME *THAT* PLUS *TEN PERCENT* TO GET YOU OFFWORLD.
MAYBE I'LL TAKE MY CHANCES WITH BOBA FETT.
YOU COULD DO THAT. WHAT ABOUT THE TRANDOSHAN BACKING HIM UP?
BOSSK'S HERE?
COME WITH ME, SOLO, AND LIVE.
WHO *ARE* YOU?
IMPERIAL CENTER SANITATION DEPARTMENT.
CALL ME *PERLA*.

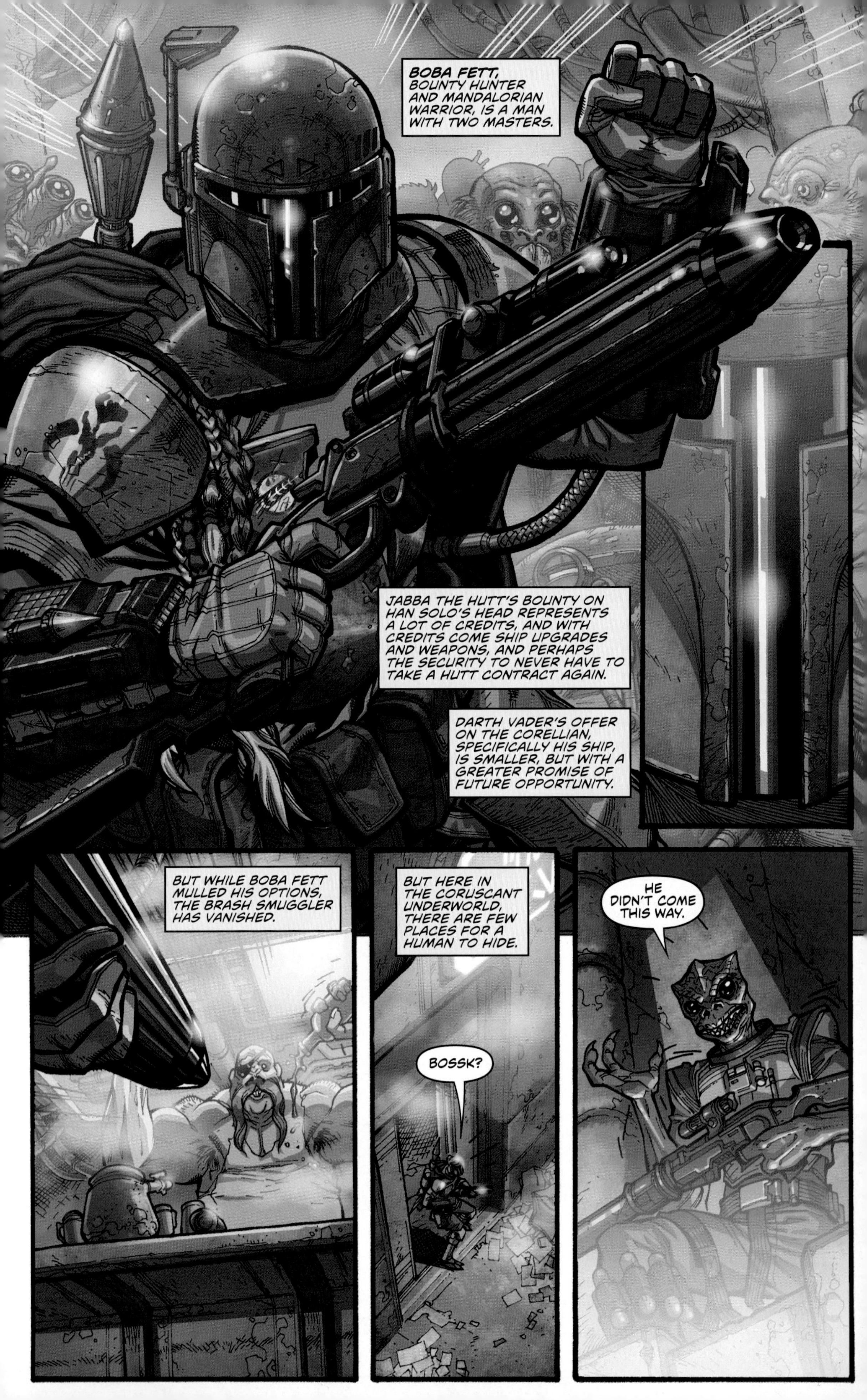
BOBA FETT, BOUNTY HUNTER AND MANDALORIAN WARRIOR, IS A MAN WITH TWO MASTERS.
JABBA THE HUTT'S BOUNTY ON HAN SOLO'S HEAD REPRESENTS A LOT OF CREDITS, AND WITH CREDITS COME SHIP UPGRADES AND WEAPONS, AND PERHAPS THE SECURITY TO NEVER HAVE TO TAKE A HUTT CONTRACT AGAIN.
DARTH VADER'S OFFER ON THE CORELLIAN, SPECIFICALLY HIS SHIP, IS SMALLER, BUT WITH A GREATER PROMISE OF FUTURE OPPORTUNITY.
BUT WHILE BOBA FETT MULLED HIS OPTIONS, THE BRASH SMUGGLER HAS VANISHED.
BUT HERE IN THE CORUSCANT UNDERWORLD, THERE ARE FEW PLACES FOR A HUMAN TO HIDE.
BOSSK?
HE DIDN'T COME THIS WAY.

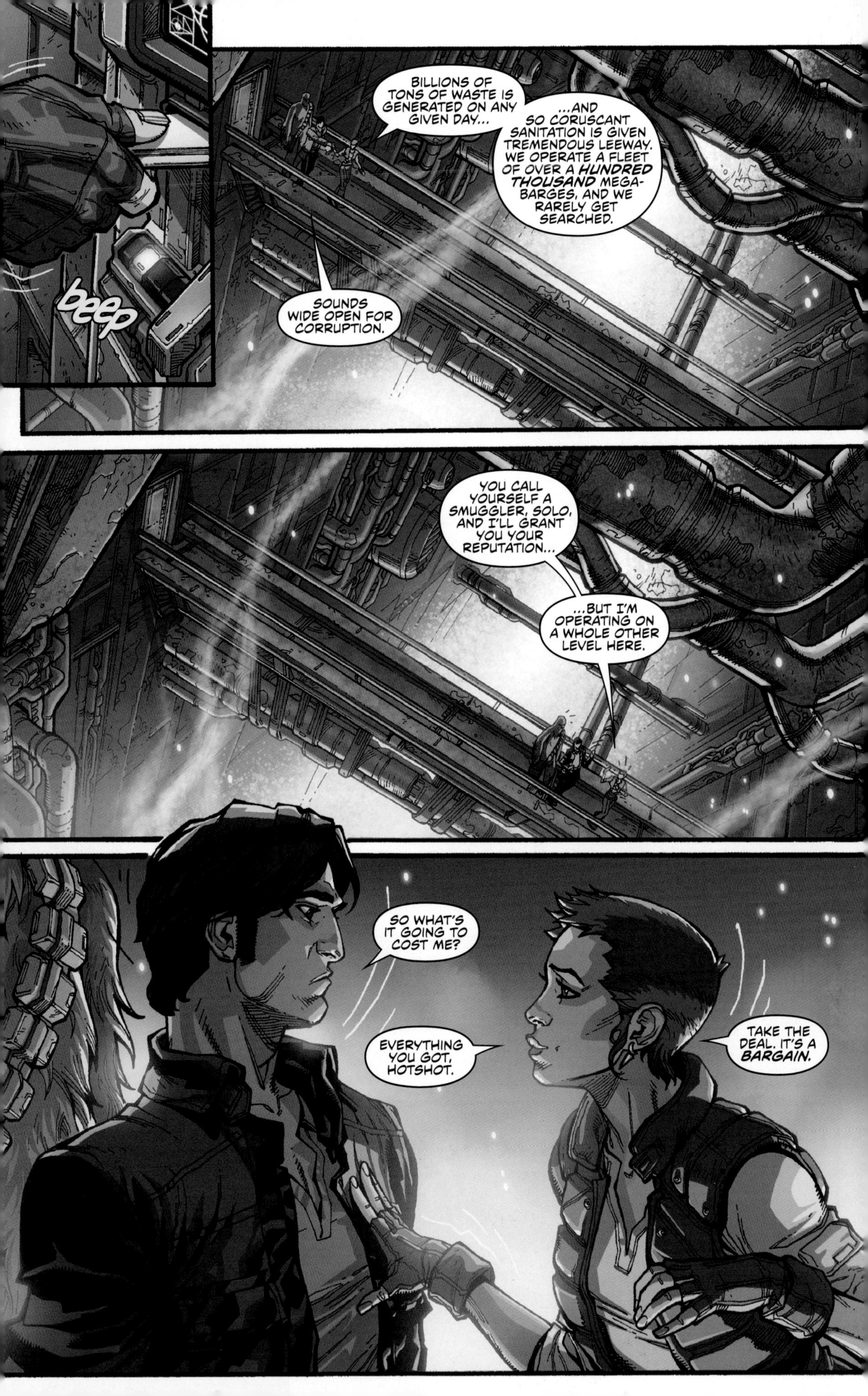
beep
BILLIONS OF TONS OF WASTE IS GENERATED ON ANY GIVEN DAY...
...AND SO CORUSCANT SANITATION IS GIVEN TREMENDOUS LEEWAY. WE OPERATE A FLEET OF OVER A HUNDRED THOUSAND MEGA-BARGES, AND WE RARELY GET SEARCHED.
SOUNDS WIDE OPEN FOR CORRUPTION.
YOU CALL YOURSELF A SMUGGLER, SOLO, AND I'LL GRANT YOU YOUR REPUTATION...
...BUT I'M OPERATING ON A WHOLE OTHER LEVEL HERE.
SO WHAT'S IT GOING TO COST ME?
EVERYTHING YOU GOT, HOTSHOT.
TAKE THE DEAL. IT'S A BARGAIN.

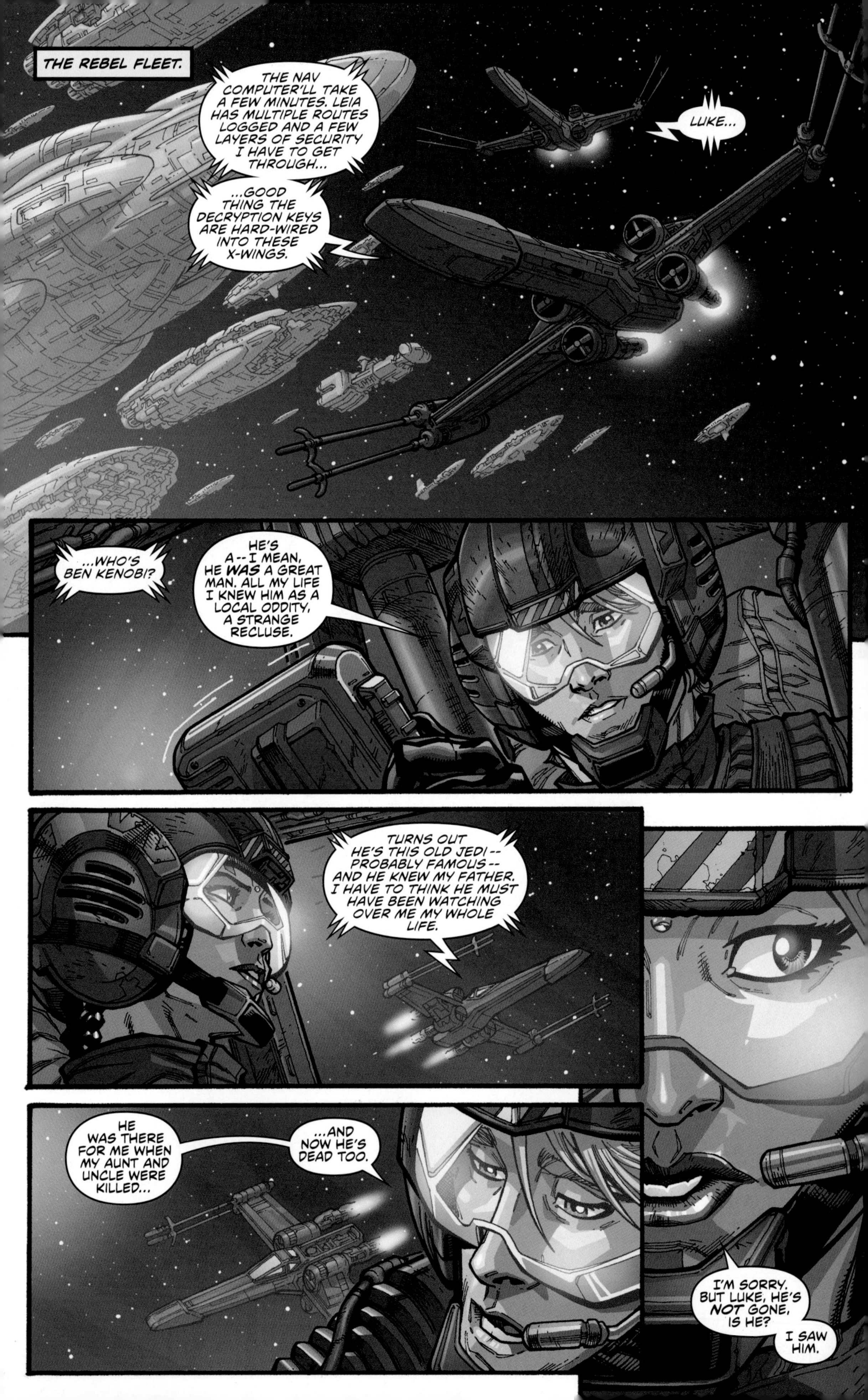
THE REBEL FLEET.
THE NAV COMPUTER'LL TAKE A FEW MINUTES. LEIA HAS MULTIPLE ROUTES LOGGED AND A FEW LAYERS OF SECURITY I HAVE TO GET THROUGH...
...GOOD THING THE DECRYPTION KEYS ARE HARD-WIRED INTO THESE X-WINGS.
LUKE...
...WHO'S BEN KENOBI?
HE'S A -- I MEAN, HE WAS A GREAT MAN. ALL MY LIFE I KNEW HIM AS A LOCAL ODDITY, A STRANGE RECLUSE.
TURNS OUT HE'S THIS OLD JEDI -- PROBABLY FAMOUS -- AND HE KNEW MY FATHER. I HAVE TO THINK HE MUST HAVE BEEN WATCHING OVER ME MY WHOLE LIFE.
HE WAS THERE FOR ME WHEN MY AUNT AND UNCLE WERE KILLED...
...AND NOW HE'S DEAD TOO.
I'M SORRY. BUT LUKE, HE'S NOT GONE, IS HE?
I SAW HIM.

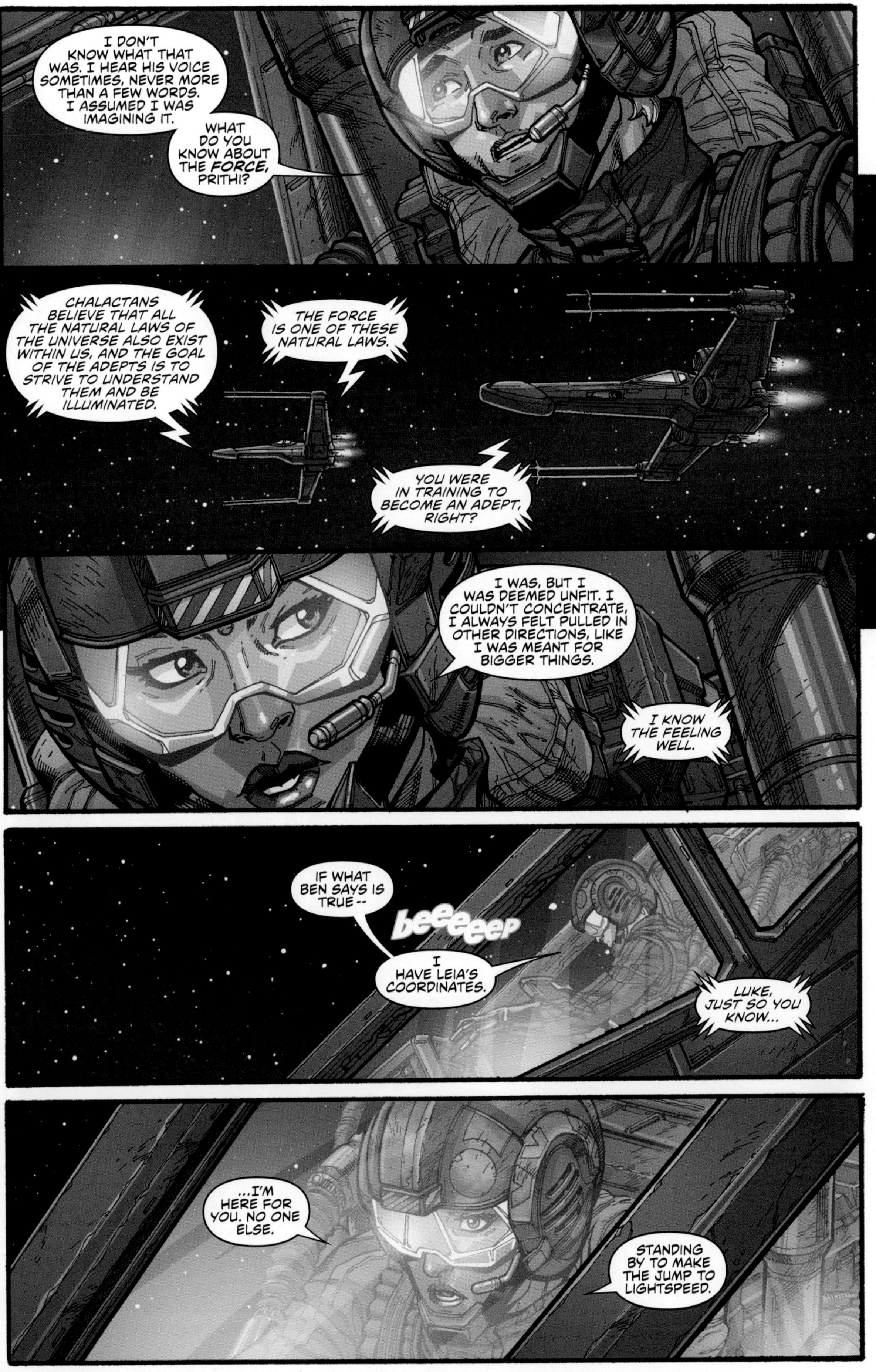
I DON'T KNOW WHAT THAT WAS. I HEAR HIS VOICE SOMETIMES, NEVER MORE THAN A FEW WORDS. I ASSUMED I WAS IMAGINING IT.
WHAT DO YOU KNOW ABOUT THE FORCE, PRITHI?
CHALACTANS BELIEVE THAT ALL THE NATURAL LAWS OF THE UNIVERSE ALSO EXIST WITHIN US, AND THE GOAL OF THE ADEPTS IS TO STRIVE TO UNDERSTAND THEM AND BE ILLUMINATED.
THE FORCE IS ONE OF THESE NATURAL LAWS.
YOU WERE IN TRAINING TO BECOME AN ADEPT, RIGHT?
I WAS, BUT I WAS DEEMED UNFIT. I COULDN'T CONCENTRATE, I ALWAYS FELT PULLED IN OTHER DIRECTIONS, LIKE I WAS MEANT FOR BIGGER THINGS.
I KNOW THE FEELING WELL.
IF WHAT BEN SAYS IS TRUE --
beeeeeep
I HAVE LEIA'S COORDINATES.
LUKE, JUST SO YOU KNOW...
...I'M HERE FOR YOU. NO ONE ELSE.
STANDING BY TO MAKE THE JUMP TO LIGHTSPEED.

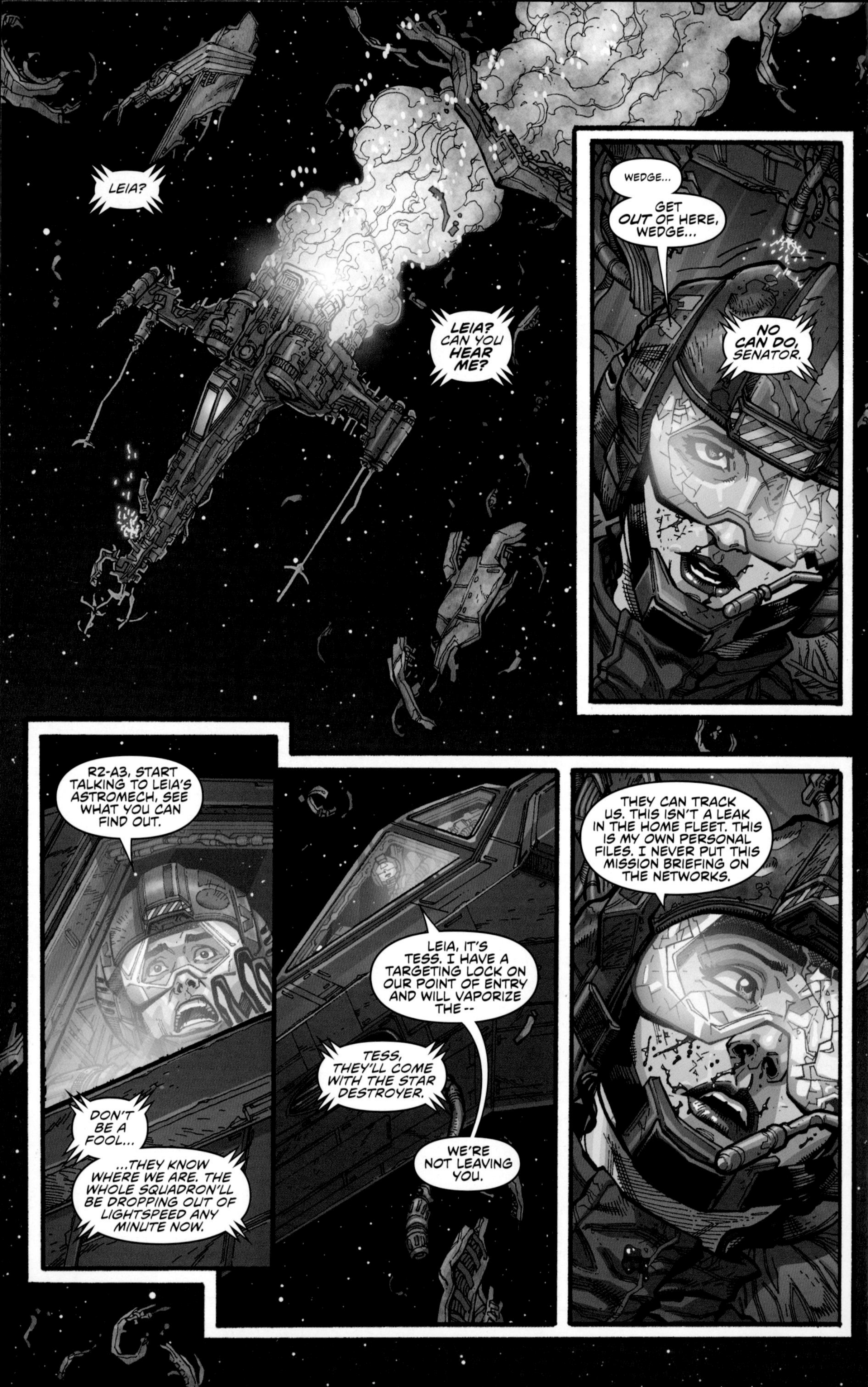
LEIA?
LEIA? CAN YOU HEAR ME?
WEDGE...
GET OUT OF HERE, WEDGE...
NO CAN DO, SENATOR.
R2-A3, START TALKING TO LEIA'S ASTROMECH, SEE WHAT YOU CAN FIND OUT.
DON'T BE A FOOL...
...THEY KNOW WHERE WE ARE. THE WHOLE SQUADRON'LL BE DROPPING OUT OF LIGHTSPEED ANY MINUTE NOW.
LEIA, IT'S TESS. I HAVE A TARGETING LOCK ON OUR POINT OF ENTRY AND WILL VAPORIZE THE --
TESS, THEY'LL COME WITH THE STAR DESTROYER.
WE'RE NOT LEAVING YOU.
THEY CAN TRACK US. THIS ISN'T A LEAK IN THE HOME FLEET. THIS IS MY OWN PERSONAL FILES. I NEVER PUT THIS MISSION BRIEFING ON THE NETWORKS.

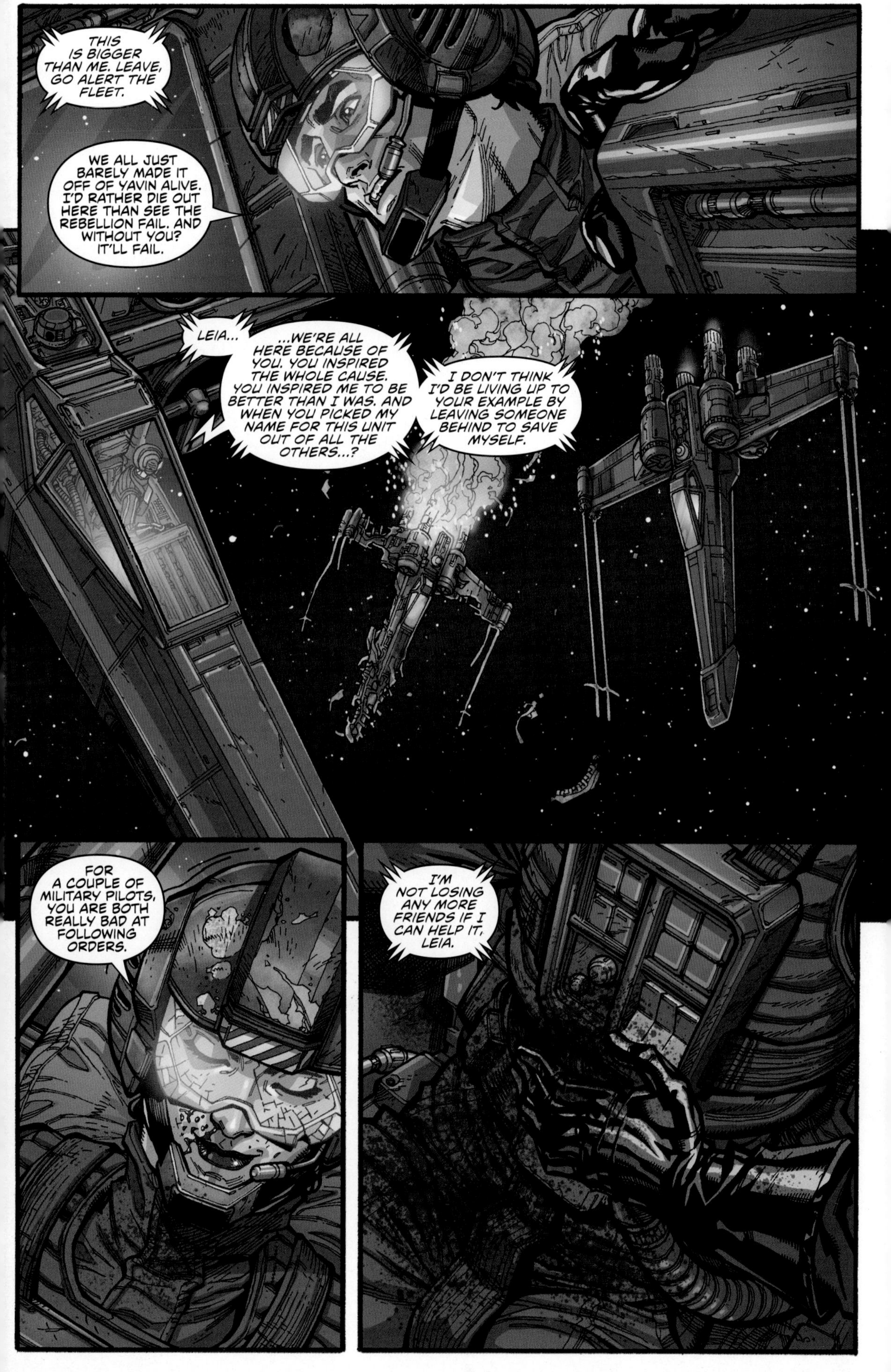
THIS IS BIGGER THAN ME. LEAVE, GO ALERT THE FLEET.
WE ALL JUST BARELY MADE IT OFF OF YAVIN ALIVE. I'D RATHER DIE OUT HERE THAN SEE THE REBELLION FAIL. AND WITHOUT YOU? IT'LL FAIL.
LEIA...
...WE'RE ALL HERE BECAUSE OF YOU. YOU INSPIRED THE WHOLE CAUSE. YOU INSPIRED ME TO BE BETTER THAN I WAS. AND WHEN YOU PICKED MY NAME FOR THIS UNIT OUT OF ALL THE OTHERS...?
I DON'T THINK I'D BE LIVING UP TO YOUR EXAMPLE BY LEAVING SOMEONE BEHIND TO SAVE MYSELF.
FOR A COUPLE OF MILITARY PILOTS, YOU ARE BOTH REALLY BAD AT FOLLOWING ORDERS.
I'M NOT LOSING ANY MORE FRIENDS IF I CAN HELP IT, LEIA.

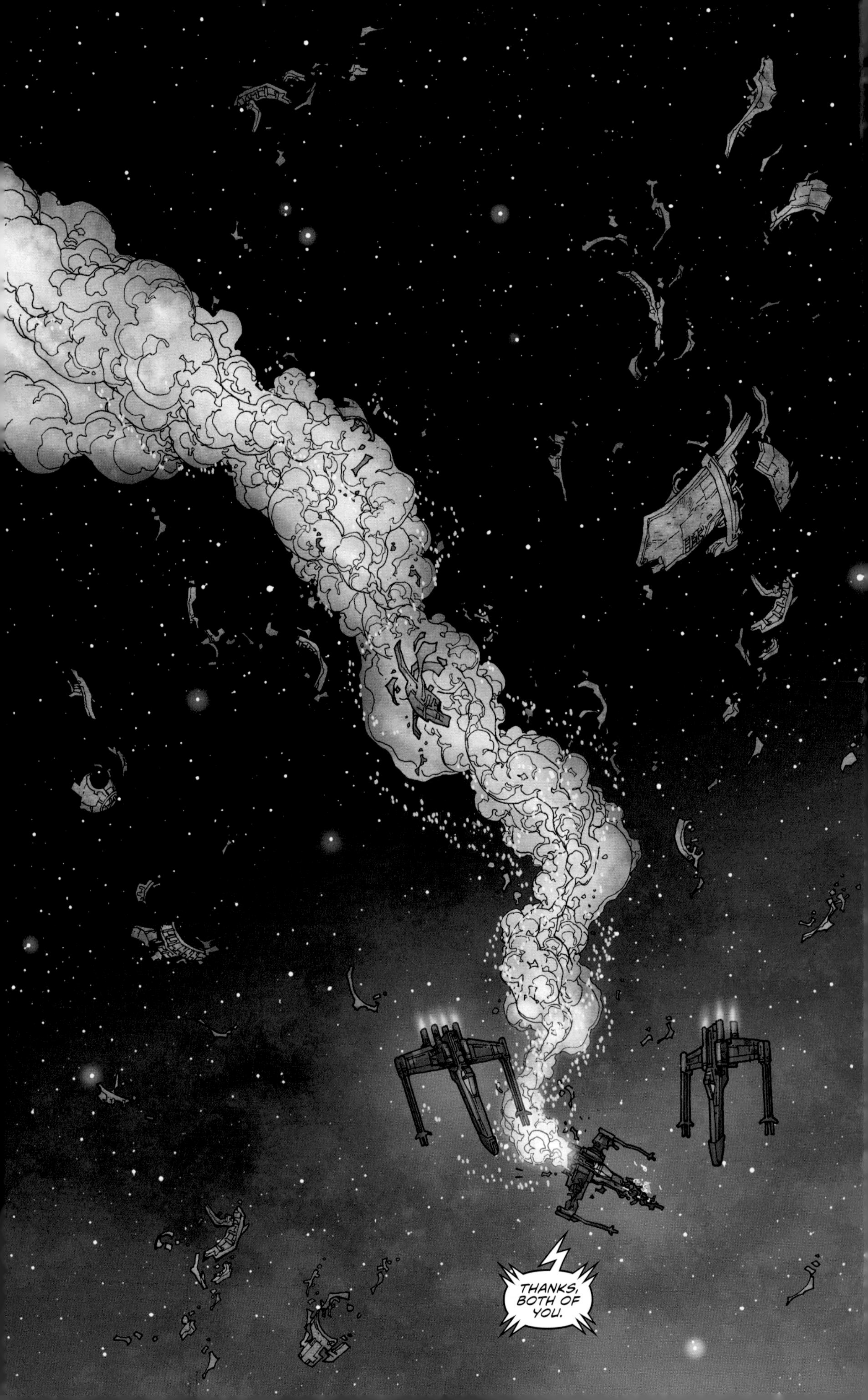
THANKS, BOTH OF YOU.

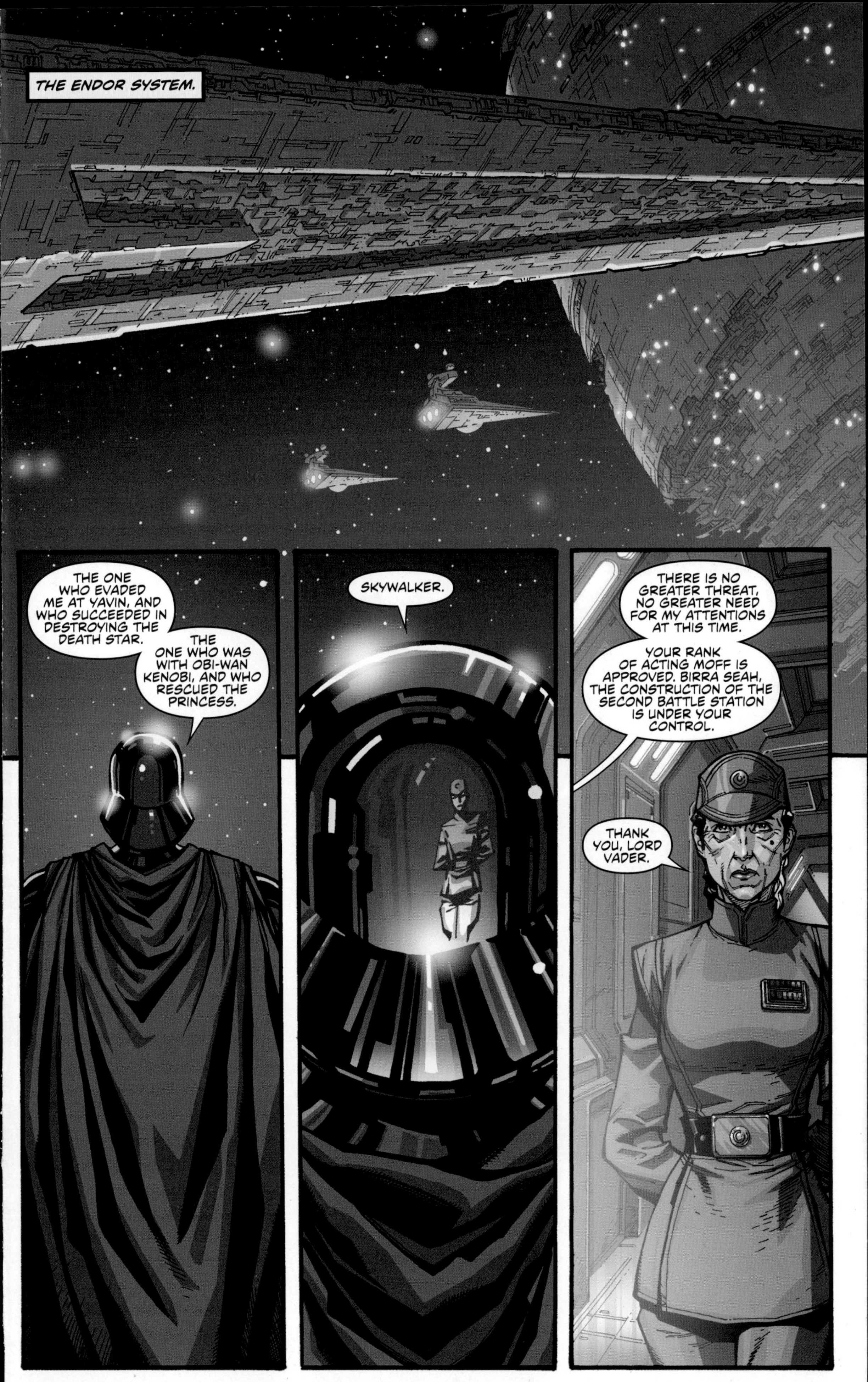
THE ENDOR SYSTEM.
THE ONE WHO EVADED ME AT YAVIN, AND WHO SUCCEEDED IN DESTROYING THE DEATH STAR.
THE ONE WHO WAS WITH OBI-WAN KENOBI, AND WHO RESCUED THE PRINCESS.
SKYWALKER.
THERE IS NO GREATER THREAT, NO GREATER NEED FOR MY ATTENTIONS AT THIS TIME.
YOUR RANK OF ACTING MOFF IS APPROVED. BIRRA SEAH, THE CONSTRUCTION OF THE SECOND BATTLE STATION IS UNDER YOUR CONTROL.
THANK YOU, LORD VADER.

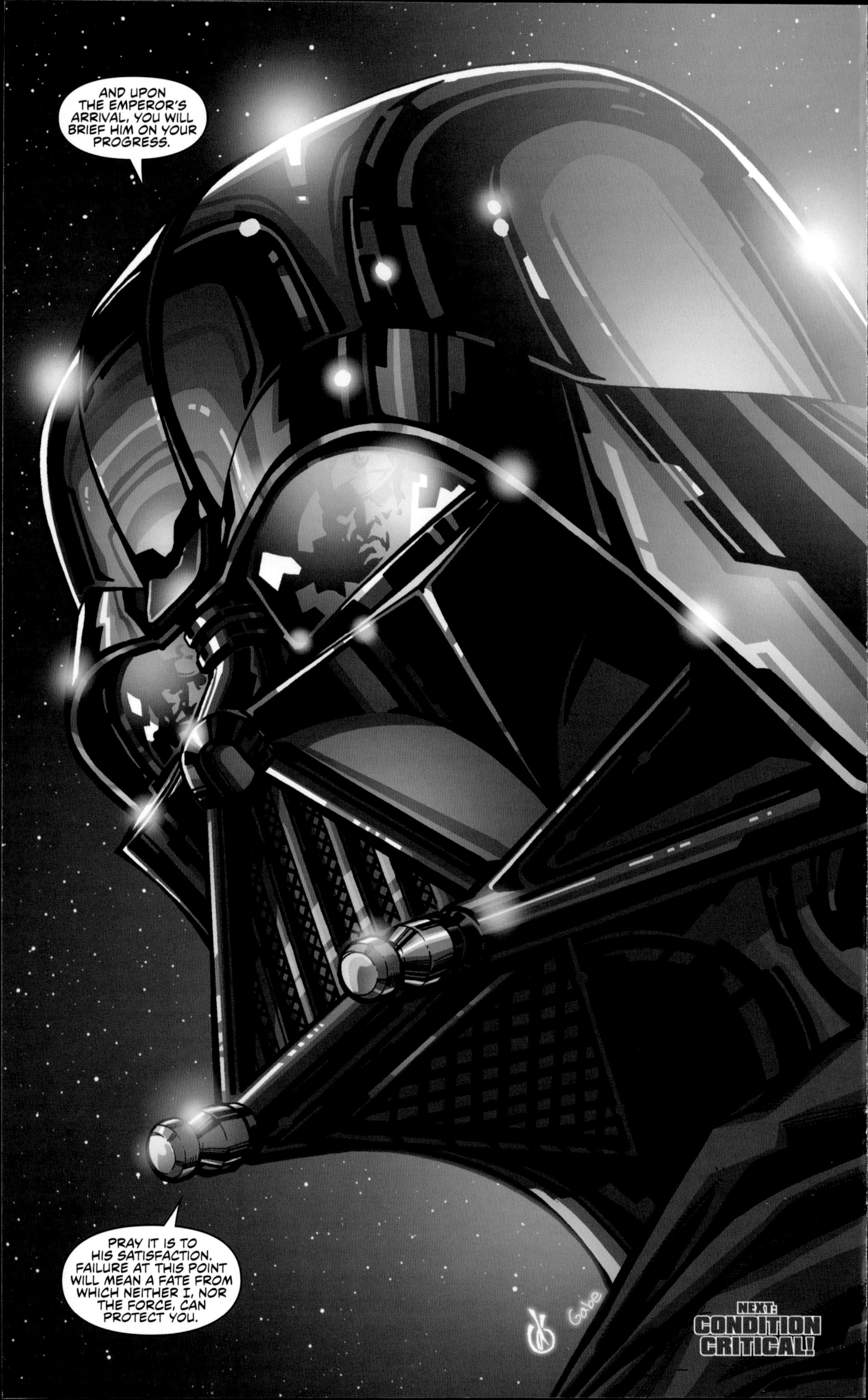
AND UPON THE EMPEROR'S ARRIVAL, YOU WILL BRIEF HIM ON YOUR PROGRESS.
PRAY IT IS TO HIS SATISFACTION. FAILURE AT THIS POINT WILL MEAN A FATE FROM WHICH NEITHER I, NOR THE FORCE, CAN PROTECT YOU.
Gabe
NEXT: CONDITION CRITICAL!